Tales of the Golden Mask

Book I

An Initiate's Tale

Large Print Edition

Alexa Lynsey and Belle De Ver

First Edition © 2017, 2020 Alexa Lynsey and Belle De Ver
Large Print Edition 2020 ISBN 9798595801720
Base cover art © rcfotostock@adobestock.com
Adapted by A. L. Butcher

Prologue

Seraphina's dark and elegant hand brushed the rough red leather of the Book of Entertainments. Her nails, gilded and long, could be both tender and devastating.

The old tome was full of mysteries to the younger members of staff at the Golden Mask, and to those who knew its contents it was a record of past glories, past assignations, and past desires. Written in the hand of at least five women and one man over the span of very many years, it had not always been in this incarnation, having had extra pages added, rebound, and at least once disguised as a book of accounts. This book had a magic of its own. Seraphina's sweeping fingers tingled and she felt the deep sensuality of knowledge and passion burn within her.

Furnished with her own taste of black and gold, a recent redecoration, the rooms were rich, comfortable and sensual. More importantly, they were now hers. She was now the premier courtesan in the city and the mistress of one of the finest Houses of Pleasure in the whole of the land. Seraphina took pride in her work, for it had given her power, wealth and freedom not enjoyed by many women in a land where they had few enough opportunities. She was not just a simple whore, she was nobility among her kind, and in this place of pleasure Seraphina was queen, spy and High Courtesan. The mask of gold gazed down from the wall, and it was said, the mask saw all and remembered much from many lives. That too had hidden in plain sight on more than one occasion but that was another tale. Now Seraphina smiled and bowed her head to it as she settled to read.

Her mother, Desiree, had taken a well-earned retirement, although, her daughter suspected, she would still entertain one or two of her more favoured clients. Desiree had been one of the most favoured concubines ever to have left the sun-blessed shores of the Far Isles and across the Silver Sea. Some of the patrons had a taste for more mature women, experience counted for a good deal in the world of pleasure. There was much to do in running an establishment such as the Golden Mask, beyond the horizontal pleasures and Desiree had a shrewd brain, many very useful contacts and did not like to be idle. Then, of course, there were the books in the library to maintain, stories, and tales to titillate, torment and tease and every one of them true. Or so Seraphina had been told.

The building which housed the Golden Mask had once been a fortress, looking out over the city proud and aloof, and it still was. Although now its walls housed those who gave and received the currency of passion and the weapons of desire. The lower rooms were dungeons of another sort. Many had paid a fortune to leave the old fortress and now, Seraphina grinned, they paid a fortune to enter.

They had plied their trade here well through the years and made powerful and influential friends; the information gained from patrons, some of whom knew not that they revealed their innermost secrets to the pretty one who lay beside them. Or that whispered promises to the talented men who gave their favours was essential in the schemes and plans of he who owned the House.

Seraphina had seen a few entries In the Book of Entertainments but there was always something new to learn. Turning past a few etchings and ink sketches at the front, she began to read the first story from those who had come before her.

A Chance Meeting

There once was a time when I was as young as I still appear to be, but I'm not sure that I was ever particularly innocent. For those who know its secrets time may be delayed, or at least the illusion of youth retained. Once I was known by a different name in a land far away. I was called Celestine, the Stargazer, and I was the junior member of the carnival dancers of Renvarik. We toured the lands and brought music, laughter, and entertainment to rich and poor alike. Soon I was to discover another form of entertainment, although some of my sisters in the carnival already knew and I would hear their giggles and sighs from beyond the caravan's canvas. In such a community one did not remain innocent for long.

Some of our kind had been blessed with magic, although in the humans this was rare, and any who were so graced had elven blood. It was not uncommon for elves and men to marry, although as I was to learn it was not always an equal partnership. Even a few generations onwards the magic would flow when a drop of elven blood flowed in one's veins. Magic had been granted to the elves, and magic goes where it pleases.

Like my mother, I had the gift of reading the stars and telling fortunes; so, while the other girls earned money for their own use with patrons after dancing on stage, I sat in the tent awaiting nightfall when those seeking good omens would arrive.

Our caravan master approved of these extra-curricular activities, for such was our reputation it paid well to supplement our skills. Gold was gold and reputation was reputation, or so he said.

One fine season the carnival master followed tales of wealth and riches to a merchant caravan travelling through the Mountains of Fire to the elven Kingdom of the Sky. We arrived late, and the festival grounds were full, but many caravans were scattered throughout the surrounding fields providing entertainment for the many travellers who could not find, or perhaps afford, lodgings within the festival village.

The caravan master had set the tents near the trees and cleared a space for dancing before the wagon. We were used to such accommodation and it did not take long to construct the makeshift stage and decorate it with fine ribbons, rich silks if we'd had a good year, and bells of bronze and copper that tinkled in the breeze. With our skin of mahogany brown, hair of wavy black that nearly reached our heels, and eyes of jet, we attracted much attention in this land of the fair-skinned High Elves, such a contrast were we to the people in this distant land. The exotic is infinitely more attractive than the familiar, a fact I was to use to my advantage in the years to come.

Many onlookers gathered about the brightly coloured tents to watch us dance that afternoon; and, for the first time, I saw a face in the crowd which stirred something in me. When he lingered by the trees with his companion at the end of the performance, I found myself milling about the back of the wagon waiting to see what he was up to.

****

"Ladies," his companion said with a bow, watching the dancing girls with great appreciation as they passed. He was the sort to appreciate the female form and his broad smile and shining eyes told us a good deal. We met many of his sort of man; confident, often generous and usually fleeting in affection.

The dancers were painted on hand and foot in intricate lace-like designs, and were covered in golden or silver jewellery everywhere; earrings, bracelets, anklets, necklaces...and other places the lads had heard as well. His eyes strained to get a peek of the nipple or thigh as the women sauntered past, flaunting themselves, teasing and tempting but not giving away more, at least not yet. A tantalising glimpse of skin, a hint of pleasures to come is a powerful tool, so I quickly learned.

We wore long, flowing skirts that wrapped into beaded head scarves, pushing up our hair until it flowed like a river. Little half- tunics left our stomachs out, curling underneath the bosom to push up and enhance. The senior girls had bright crimson, and the juniors among us wore autumn colours of gold and orange made from fine silks and linens from faraway lands. Some dancers had painting or jewels around their navels, jewels which caught the light and drew the eye.

What have we here?" said one dancer as she trailed her hand down the first lad's arm playfully. "I don't recall seeing you in camp last night, I would remember someone that looked like you." She winked at the others, who stifled giggles.

The lad who had caught my eye blushed, his very pale skin reddening deeply, his bluish-white hair intensifying the look. He was fascinating. His companion was shorter and darker in colouration, with hair of strawberry and skin of peaches and cream. Between them was found a strong resemblance, the same shape of eye, and cast of jaw. They could be related, I thought but said nothing.

The bolder of the two young men smiled as he answered the girls, "We weren't in camp last night, but after seeing you dance today, we wanted to meet you. Perhaps get to know you a little better..." The shy one nodded but was not nearly as forward as his companion.

"Oh, I see," said another dancer as she stepped up to him and slid her arm through his.

"Were you hoping for a private showing then?" she smiled as she slid the scarf from her hair to dangle down her back, caught in the crook of her elbows. A throaty chuckle made the fairer young man blush again.

"Don't tease them so Leela," another girl admonished as she paused at the flap of the tent. "Look at their belts. They've not got a purse between them."

"Only a fool would string his purse on his belt in this crowd," the dark one insisted as he stood up straighter, jingling the pocket of his waistcoat. "I've coins yet to be spent today. Besides, we can take care of ourselves."

"Do you now, and can you?" asked the dancer who had been flirting with the young man I couldn't stop watching. "I do believe yours is hoping to see the dance again and bask in our beauty." She winked at her friend and waggled her hips towards him.

"I believe he's hoping for a little of what comes after the dance," Leela teased as she ran a finger across the dark one's cheek and down his throat, slowly pulling at the knot where his tunic was laced closed. A sharp intake of breath from her new friend made Leela, slither ever closer. "Hopeful, are we?" Her voice was sultry in his ear.

"Do you know who they are?" one of the workmen hissed as Nisha grinned and one painted finger traced the line of Skylon's jaw.

"Lads with curious minds?" one of the older dancers teased, enjoyed the show.

"They're from the High Palace," the workman warned as he hefted the chest. "Mind yourselves and send those fellows home, they are not for the likes of you," he commanded before heading towards the festival village.

"Don't mind him," said the dark one. "I'm known as Dorien, and this is my twin brother Skylon, and we're bored with the festival. We wanted to see what goes on outside of the palace. Our... duties are done."

"Twins, is it?" Nisha whispered in Skylon's ear. "And do you do everything together?" Nisha's voice was sultry, full of desire as she looked from one brother to the other.

"Yes," Dorien replied breathlessly as Leela began to unwrap the impossibly long scarf from around her waist until nothing was left save a small triangle of linen tied on by cords. Tossing the cloth into the tent she took his hand and walked into the trees. Skylon watched her lead Dorien away, who cast a grin over his shoulder.

Skylon rolled his eyes. Dorien was always so impetuous, so bold. It had caused trouble in the past and no doubt would again. It had been his idea to lose their escort in the crowd and Dorien's pleading with their father to let them see the festival. Nisha chuckled and let her fingers walk down his chest to pause, temptingly at the belt of his breeches.

Nisha grinned, "Sensible fellow…now, master Skylon how may the ladies of the Bright Caravan serve you?"

****

We knew some caravan masters allowed the younger girls to be taken as 'consorts', but ours decreed seventeen or eighteen winters of age must have passed at least. It was the law in several of the provinces, and he was a cautious man. It was not through any moral obligation – simply he did not wish to be arrested by the constables and justices. He decreed also that the 'special herbs' must be used to prevent disease and unwanted pregnancy. After all, a pregnant girl, couldn't dance.

Leela was an experienced dancer and an excellent lover, or so I had been told. Her earnings ensured hers was the most luxurious caravan, and the finest costumes graced her splendid form.

Nisha still gripped Skylon's hand, and then took mine, winking and whispering, "Let us go and watch, it will be an education for you and for him. He is not so bold as his brother…Soon you are due to become a consort." Her tongue darted out, like the emerald lizards who sometimes took up residence in the tents. Then ran over dark, plum-painted lips. She enjoyed such thoughts, and 'breaking in' initiates brought her a good deal of pleasure; I was, perhaps too inexperienced then to understand it, but I could see the wicked gleam in her eyes.

Before I could answer and ask how she knew Skylon was uneducated in such matters, she kissed me, lingering her lips on mine. "Curiosity is so becoming, Celestine, now no arguments. It will serve you well enough."

With a sly look to Skylon, whose eyes flicked from my face to Nisha's and back again, lingering on my dark skin, and wide eyes, she leaned towards my ear, "Look how he stares at you… a man from the palace, it's you he desires… I'll simply warm him up…. Perhaps we can arrange the 'maiden-price' for you. He might have a wealthy father who indulges his son before his wedding. The Caravan Master will agree if the young man's coin is good enough."

I was not yet initiated into that sort of entertainment but I was curious. It never hurt to learn a few tricks from the masters, or in this case mistresses. What she said was true… the 'maiden-price' could be high for the comeliest of us. Those most sought after. Many of the dancers never officially received the 'maiden-price', and amongst the troupe, those who did were more respected, more admired.

We crept through the trees to the clearing, the girls had scoped out such a useful patch of ground the morning we arrived. A little more private than a tent in a crowded festival ground, but easy to access and enough patches of trees for those who revel in watching such past-times.

Dorien sprawled on a pallet in a small, cleared away space not far from the camp. Leela lay across him, Dorien's breeches open and his swollen member in her mouth. He held her tightly about the waist as he buried his face in her sweetness, moaning at the sheer delight of her taste. It was not his first experience of the charms of women and he knew what he liked. The sounds of passion on the breeze carrying to our hiding place. I felt the heat of desire, the warm tingle beneath my saffron costume and saw the fiery gleam in Nisha's eyes. Her lips moistened as she ran her tongue slowly along then, casting a glance towards Skylon, whose eyes were riveted on the glade.

Skylon stood and watched, entranced by the scene. Nisha whispered in his ear, "Everything together…would you share her today, or shall I pleasure you while you watch him take his fill?"

Nisha slowly backed Skylon against a tree, "Don't you worry; you'll enjoy someone soon enough. Maybe just a taste then...something to leave you thinking on it, wishing you had taken more?"

Slowly she unwrapped the orange cloth she wore and let it pool at her feet. She lifted the little half shirt over her head until she was dressed in nothing but gold. Two golden stars covered her nipples, connected by a gold chain. Several more chains hung about her hips, the little stars on those jingled as she started to shake her hips in front of him. The bangles on her arms and ankles jingled, the sounds blending with the moans from Dorien and Leela, almost hypnotic. Skylon's heart raced and his blood boiled until the pain in his cock made him slide down the tree squatting in the dirt against the trunk, watching as Leela pumped Dorien.

Nisha pushed his legs apart and sat in his lap, smothering Skylon with hungry kisses. She rubbed herself over him. He could feel the heat of her, the wetness through the linen of his breeches. He moaned as she rubbed faster and faster. Yet his eyes moved to me, watching as I squirmed with need. Watching as my fingers quested downwards, beneath my skirt. I may never have bedded a man but that did not mean I was entirely inexperienced in the ways of pleasure. After all, we soon gained far more knowledge of what was expected of us than a peasant girl, or shy noble bride. Ours was a small society, where secrets and skills were shared. Not one of us remained innocent for long.

We cried out together, reaching our peaks as one, and Nisha whispered in Skylon's ear, "Apparently, you two really do everything together!"

She kissed him again before picking up her clothing and making a small bundle of it. "I hope to see you before the fire tonight, for I'll take you first if you come." She winked at him and wandered off through the trees, casting me a grin and a nod. "Time to return, Stargazer, there is much to do, and many more nights to seek pleasure." With a quick gesture, she touched my damp fingers to my cheek. "He watches you, young one. It's I who brought him off but it's you he thought of, trust me."

With that, she motioned me back to camp. Grinning with that knowing smile many of the older women often had.

As Leela sat up, Dorien rolled, hands still about her waist, and landed her on the pallet, "Oh no," he chuckled, "I'm not done with you yet." He turned around, sitting astride her, and took her wrists in his hands, holding her to the mat.

"You would have more of me, my lord?" she whispered, a smile playing about her lips.

"Yes," he answered, voice still husky with passion.

"Then take what you desire from me," she replied as she lifted her head to kiss him.

"We should return, you'll be missed. Have you somewhere I could clean up? My father is going to kill us. We'll be confined in the Palace until we are thirty!" Skylon muttered to me, his blue eyes never leaving mine.

Now the heat of passion was sated he looked rather dishevelled and embarrassed to have tumbled with Nisha. There was something about this young man, an intensity, and a sadness. Perhaps he lived in his brother's shadow. I knew what it was to be the junior, the second best. That afternoon my life took a new track as I took pity on a young man, who, in other circumstances, I might have simply ignored, or done as the other girls did and moved on.

There were clean clothes in a chest beneath one of the benches and I filled a small stone bowl with water from the pitcher, scenting it with fragrant and heady oils from the lands far to the West. I rummaged until I found the best pair of breeches I could, sky blue and white diamonds and, with a smile at his embarrassment, I turned my back whilst he dressed. After what he'd just done I found it amusing, and rather enchanting. We kept some clothes both for disguise and the male dancers who would sometimes join us. I'd been mending them, and would likely have to account for the loss – but perhaps if Skylon were to accidently leave his own behind, then washed and dried recompense would be found.

"Nisha rarely takes no for an answer. You are lucky, she's an experienced consort. Your brother too, he sports with one of our best. Both can be rather…. overwhelming. Many young men have fallen beneath both their spells. Sometimes they work together and their prey has little chance of resistance. It's a kind of magic you know, a kind of primal need they turn to their advantage. Magic is everywhere about us. It shows itself in many ways and passion is their magic. Sex is power, so they say. Apparently, it makes them better dancers. All that… er, energy and desire channelled in a different way. They are very good at what they do. Do not be ashamed, you're not the first and I doubt you'll be the last. Nisha seeks out the…uninitiated as she calls them."

Skylon managed a smile, this young woman seemed different to the others, far kinder, and more intense, he thought. There was something about her, a depth he hadn't seen in the rather forward dancers who'd been so forthcoming with their favours.

As it was we talked as the sun made its inexorable journey across the sky. He watched and even helped me as I began to sew and mend. I felt his fascination with me, and the gentleness in him. After what seemed a lifetime but at the same time much too soon Dorien called to him, "Brother – get you from the wench's wagon. We'll be missed, it's time to go."

****

That chance meeting was the beginning of a new and beautiful time in my life, and one I will never regret following. That evening the two young men returned to me, riding in a litter of gold, and served by an entourage of finely attired men and women. Later I was to learn that this had been their first excursion without an escort, their first festival as adults and heirs to the kingdom. I had thought them sons of some minor courtiers, rich and well-bred but never in my wildest dreams had I expected them to return, or to be princes of this realm. Sometimes the consorts spent several nights or afternoons with the same patrons and rarely they were taken from the troupe and set up as a mistress but I had never imagined it would be me. Of all the dancers and consorts I had expected Leela or Nisha to be so honoured. In my younger, less worldly days I never thought to ask what happened to such women when their patrons grew tired of them.

A man wearing robes of amethyst and holding a papyrus scroll stepped from the litter. Two burly gentlemen walked forward with a small banded chest and set it before our caravan master. One of the porters knelt, unlocked the chest, and casually lifted the lid. It appeared to contain the entire wealth of the merchants we had followed here. Never had I seen such coin.

"The Prince of the Snowy Sky wishes the Reader of Stars to join him at the High Palace. He offers this token as assurance she will be cared for and adored. He asks for your assurance that none others lay claim to her now, or in the future."

The Caravan Master had a love of gold beyond his fondness for his dancers, after all, we could be replaced, although it was not a life suited to all. Many girls came and failed in the acrobatics, and the long and hard physical requirements. Such girls were either kept on as simple servants; scrubbing, and cleaning the caravans and tents, hauling water and tending the animals if they were pretty or simply abandoned at the nearest available village if they weren't comely enough to earn their keep on their backs. It was not an easy life, but then, I suppose we didn't ask questions. I assumed the girls were bought or given to the caravans - such was the way of things then. Boys too, on occasion would come our way. In a world where every extra mouth to feed was an added burdon for those already on the edge of poverty a family would oft 'gift' a daughter or younger son. Sometimes those who had reason to be ever on the move would join us as guard, stagehand or driver. Tents and stages did not erect themselves. In my latter years and life I knew the value of such people – who asked no questions, could move un-noticed, and more importantly listened and watched. That, however, is a different tale.

Our master hid his surprise at the choice of the rich young men well. He too had assumed Nisha or Leela or another of the most experienced dancers would be chosen. I learned later that an envoy had come from the palace to discuss the acquisition of some of the troupe, being the man he was, the master haggled. Skylon told me the man mentioned my humble origins, my lack of father but on that glorious evening he signed the scroll in his own blood and rescinded all knowledge and care of me. Who I was, who I had been and who I would become belonged now to another.

The last thing I saw as the porter lifted me into the litter was Leela's mouth open in shock and envy. As the curtains closed I heard the caravan master's voice for the last time, "The festival has been so profitable. I think it is finally time that we should return to our homeland."

The Painted Lady

The golden litter arrived before a sprawling old townhouse at the far edge of the high district within the festival village, its grand spires towering high into the sky I had spotted long before we arrived. Four stories not counting the towers, the house all but glowed like the morning sun, painted in the colours of dawn in a city where greys and browns predominated the landscape. The door was the one dark spot on the entire building, painted a deep eggplant with the twin masks of gold denoting players, a symbol I was more than familiar with from my caravan travels. Perhaps I was mistaken in the young men's intentions. Perhaps I would simply be a dancer, or given to someone else.

Standing on the cobbles before the Painted Lady, as I was soon to learn the establishment was known, was a truly handsome gentleman, being tall and slender with long, silvery-white hair and a sculptured face. His ears were finely pointed, set with gems running the length of them, as I had heard was fashionable among the elves. The hand he held out for me was be-ringed with amber and gold. And his grip was strong yet gentle. He resembled a statue I had once seen in a temple, in a far-off town. My two escorts seemed confused as to where we were and what was going on, and for a moment I feared for our safety until that mysterious man's silver eyes held mine, and with a smile, he lifted me from the carriage and bid me follow him. I felt safe with him, and slyly and shyly cast my glances over him. He resembled most the Prince Skylon, with his pale looks and hair. If this man was to be my destiny I could do much worse. Besides, it was hardly my place to complain.

The excitement of the evening had ebbed to a feeling of nervousness during our journey. Skylon had been trying to reassure me and Dorien, well Dorien talked mostly about the palace and himself. He was not unkind but he was rather aloof. To him I was simply a dancing girl, I was wise enough to know he probably did not even think about Nisha. He'd had a taste of pleasure and I learned he had also been pleasured by Leela when I was with his brother in the wagon. The brothers were very different it seemed.

I was in a strange town, with men I barely knew. I had very little money of my own and I spoke some but not all of their language. Suddenly I felt very young, very alone and not nearly as cocky as I had when I had grinned at Leela's jealousy. It was, however, too late to do much about it. I'd always known the dancers and servants of the Caravan Master had been purchased. I realised now we were whores in all but name. The old master had not been unkind or cruel, at least not be the standards of some. We had often talked with other women such as ourselves and I'd even been told of dancers being caged when they weren't working to stop them running away. I'd been lucky, although we worked hard and being part of a travelling troupe was a life largely of being slightly cold and hungry, never making friends beyond the troupe or settling roots it was, for my part, no worse than the life I would have had otherwise. Working in the fields or at the mill from sunup to sundown and popping out a baby every year. I was a good dancer, and acrobatic. I could juggle, sing and even ride the stout ponies. I was a good seamstress, could read and write well enough and what money we earned beyond the dancing mostly we could keep. We were tended when we were ill or injured and saw far more of the world than most. Yet a little voice in my head asked 'What now? Would I miss my dancing sisters, and our wagons?'

Seeing the fear in my eyes the elven lord smiled, "Welcome Celestine, Gazer and Reader of Stars. Welcome to the Kingdom of the Sky and the city of Aura. I have heard much of your talents and kindness to my son. I am Lucius, lord of this land."

Dorien snorted, "That's one way of putting it."

Skylon squeezed my hand and helped me from the litter. "Ignore him. He thinks of nothing but his own pleasures. He isn't a bad person... just a bit self-obsessed."

"Self-obsessed? Me? I don't know what you mean," Dorien glared at his brother.

Skylon grinned, pushing his brother good-naturedly. "I know you don't, dear brother. You are a charming rogue and far surer of yourself than I. I just think you could be a little less... blatant."

With a cough, Lucius reminded them who they were, and where.

Prince Dorien looked around with arms crossed eyeing the colourful building before us. "A playhouse? Father, why have you had us brought to a playhouse? I'm certain that Skylon wishes to get his little pet..."

His father coughed again, and an eyebrow lifted as he patted my arm, that had been braver than the rest of me and slid onto this enigmatic lord's arm "Concubine...he has acquired his first concubine or consort. I have already sent word ahead that your rooms should be moved and a new wing opened in the Zenana. It wouldn't do for your ladies to be mingled with mine. Although this one is quite delightful. Such an intriguing tone of skin, and enchanting figure. Skylon always was the one to desire the exotic and unusual."

"This seems an odd place for a playhouse," Skylon noted. "It doesn't much look like the playhouse near the festival centre."

Lord Lucius chuckled, "My dear sons, you will learn soon enough that appearances can be deceptive."

A man passed them on the cobbles, hood pulled over his head, a golden half-mask obscuring his face. He paused and regarded the new arrivals, "Ah, a different sort of playhouse it is to be certain. One filled with entertainments for the... discriminating gentleman." He bowed to them and continued, opening the door with a jewelled key and entering.

The brothers looked first to one another, and then to their father who simply smiled, "Some men feel a need for a bit of drama and mystery. They believe it to enhance the experience.

You will find this playhouse always provides exactly the show you wanted to see, and you will never leave disappointed. Sometimes one must leave the Zenana. It is exciting and useful to be a man-about-town. One can learn a great deal of intrigue and politics in such a place as this. One's disguise is anonymity, wealth, and desire; they are also one's strengths and weaknesses. Choose wisely how to use them."

With a wave, Lucius dismissed the litter, it was obvious the litter bearers were used to this routine. Removing a golden key, and three masks from the recesses of his cloak Lucius unlocked the door and led them inside, without another word.

"I'm still confused. All this intrigue makes my head spin," Dorien grumbled, eyeing his brother whose fingers were woven into mine.

I dared not speak, for what did a dancer know of intrigue and politics and I did not wish to disgrace myself. I would learn soon enough the power of desire, the power that a woman may hold over a man. I was, in essence, a slave, although that too I didn't truly understand until later and when I discovered that fact I knew I would never be a slave again, unless it suited my purpose. Within these walls, and the walls of the Zenana, it was often the men who were slaves to their desire and the women. On that day, I held my tongue, my eyes roaming from Lord Lucius to his two sons and back again. I was a pawn in a game, and I didn't understand the rules. Not then.

Skylon muttered, "We both best learn it, we will have use of it. Why do you think Father has survived so long? He's cleverer, more devious and has more spies than his rivals. He sweetens them with good wine, beautiful women, and fine items. It's a good strategy."

The reception parlour of the playhouse was grand, with bright crimson brocade and velvet trimmed with gold braid. Tall statues of men and women cavorting stood at the edge of each curtained recess, and each statue was naked. Such richness I had never seen, being used to the faded canvas of our tents and caravans. Even when we had stopped in towns never had we been such a place as this.

Benches covered in silk and high-backed chairs of jet back wood were scattered around, some facing one another, some against the wall. A tall, comely woman with skin darker than even my own and lips as red as blood, bowed to Lucius and as he reached to brush his lips across her cheek he murmured, "Tatia!"

A mask painted gold and adorned with tall black feathers obscured part of the woman's face, making her mysterious. Yet it was obvious Lucius visited this place often enough to know who was whom. I could not tell the age of this woman, partly due to her mask but partly because her ears were slightly pointed, noting her elven heritage. I knew the islands and lands east of the Far Isles, the land of my birth, produced people of her colouring, but I was surprised to see one here. In the few years, I had spent there I encountered few of the elven race.

How may we serve you today, Highness?"

"How fares your mother, my dear? It has been some time since I've seen her," he asked as he took her arm and wrapped his hand around hers, patting it softly as they moved towards the back of the house. A quick snap of Tatia's fingers and one of the ladies waiting at the top of the stairs quickly took her place on the couch. A gentle nudge from a shadowy figure which had seemingly materialised behind them sent the lads hurriedly through the parlour and down the hall after their father, my hand firmly gripped in Skylon's. Dorien looked quizzically up the stairway as they walked past before glancing over his shoulder to sneak one more glimpse of the ladies sitting in the parlour.

We found ourselves in a comfortable sitting room decorated with plush chairs, lounging couches, and pillows. Scented candles and lamps contained in coloured glass jars cast a soft and rather sensual light around the room. Two doors opened to either side of the room revealing boudoirs with high canopy beds. A third door, directly before us, was closed. There was no mistaking what this place was. A house of pleasure!

Dorien was craning his neck, trying to catch a glimpse of the girls we had seen before and Skylon looked a little uncomfortable. Me, I had never seen a place quite this opulent, or unashamed of what it was, but one of my former colleagues among the caravan dancers had told me of a wealthy pleasure house in a city at the edge of the Silver Sea. The women there served both men and other women and a successful courtesan could retire a very wealthy woman, with servants of her own and no need for any man's keeping but those she now chose.

"It was good to hear that you are managing things now. Your mother has worked long and hard to get where she is," his majesty commented to his companion as he looked about the room.

Tatia laughed, "She only entertains when it pleases her, and only for the most distinguished of clients. She manages to keep herself busy with her books, magic, and art. You would be impressed with how the library has grown. Most of the consorts acquire an education and when they leave, they can make their own way in the world. Mariana, the elven consort from the Silver Isles has left to run a fine house – governess to a lord's children and housekeeper to a fine man. She has no shame attached to her time here, a simple hunter's daughter who could neither read nor write when she arrived at fifteen winters and now she has wealth, status, and respect.

"Mother is quite the diplomat these days. She spends many evenings with important personages and their wives. She says it's amazing the gossip people let slip, particularly to a beautiful woman. She was hoping to send you some…. information, lord, but perhaps she would prefer to divulge it in person. You need no invitation to her chambers."

"I wish to entrust to her a precious gift, a gemstone in the rough. I know she can shape it to bring out all the best qualities. She is still the most gifted of artisans in that sphere. Those fingers, which can coax the light from the dark, the smooth from the rough... and drive a man almost to madness with desire." Lucius smiled, fond in his memory.

"For you, Majesty, I am certain she will do this, but perhaps you would enjoy visiting with her yourself? I happen to know a hot bath has just been drawn and a meal ordered from the kitchens," Tatia winked as she bowed low, her outstretched hand offering the closed door at the end of the room. "I am sure she would love to renew a fond and valued acquaintance."

"Indeed," he smiled broadly as he nodded his head. "Then I entrust into your care these boys - my sons. They seem to have had a brief glimpse of...entertainment at the festival. I leave you to decide the best means to...occupy them while I am behind closed doors. Broaden their education before they take up their duties, you might say."

Tatia tugged a cord hanging near the door of the chamber, and within moments a young woman in a pale blue tunic arrived. Suddenly attention was on me, and I found myself being scrutinised as I was led away from Skylon towards a curtain. With a swift motion, Tatia pulled back the curtain to reveal the largest and shiniest looking glass I had ever seen. Some of the dancers had owned them, but they were little more than polished copper or stone. This oval beauty was as tall as I was and as broad as a man's span. I remember now standing with my mouth agape.

"What is your name, girl?" Tatia tilted my chin, turned me this way and that and ran one hand slowly along my leg and behind, as though appraising a cow or pony.

The sale of pretty lads and girls was not unusual as I well knew, but I was still apprehensive. My heart fluttered nervously and I tried not to stutter as I replied, "Celestine, mistress."

"A good match for our Prince of the Snowy Sky, and I feel a spark within you...you wield the power of the ancients? Your blood is blessed, girl. The Goddess favours you."

"I am a Stargazer, mistress; but the omens do not appear as often as I was bid seek them," I replied, cautiously and rather embarrassed at my failings.

"They never do, child. They never do. I will send to the Guild for the proper tutor, for that is a skill we cannot teach. Treela, please take our guest to the apprentice quarters. Please be sure she has a warm bath, a hot meal and soft clothes. Madam will send for her when the contract has been settled." With that, she tapped the mirror and commanded, "Remember this girl, Celestine. Show her when bidden."

That was when I learned that even a mirror may be magical, as it rippled and the most incredible feeling of intensity filled me. Every part of my body tingled, and as I caught my breath I wondered what more could it do. Later I would learn, for now, I yearned for the pounding in my quim to be sated. As I stood there Seraphina smirked, "You'll soon learn, a reader of stars, you'll soon learn."

I stared at Treela, for she had never seen a girl who looked such. While the residents of this land mostly seemed to be tall, willowy, and pale as clouds, this girl was dark, but not in the way of the desert people or the ebony woman like Tatia. Treela's skin was greyer, like slate and her hair wiry and a bright blue, not fluffy like Tatia's, and above her ears, the girl had horns like a ram, decorated with rings of silver and bronze. Before I could even think of a question to ask about such oddities, Skylon called out as I was led away.

"Wait!" demanded Skylon. "Where is she going?"

"Why, to be trained properly for you, dear Prince," Tatia replied smiling sweetly.

"No one is to touch her," he replied, voice soft and eyes squinted, "not even a servant. She is for my touch alone."

"As you wish," Tatia answered, her cocked brow silently asking his father's opinion.

His majesty chuckled and shook his head, "She is a concubine. If he wishes to train her, so be it. I shall place it in her contract. Considering that, I think one month should do for her...tutelage in your library. Send the Guild tutor to the High Palace when you deliver her."

He started for the door and then paused. "I think, perhaps, the Prince of the Snowy Sky should stay as well. Perhaps it is he who should discover what he likes so that he can train his concubine." Kissing Tatia's hand, he strolled through the closed door as though the rooms were his own.

"Hey, wait a minute!" Dorien objected as the metallic click of a lock was heard from the now-closed door. "What about me? He barely even opened his drawers for the dancing girls."

"Never you fear, Prince Dorien you will not be left out," Tatia snickered softly as she guided the boys back towards the front parlour.

****

I'm sure at the time two frustrated young princes were confused and rather annoyed. Dorien certainly enjoyed a chase and here he was surrounded by women vastly more experienced, here he was the novice. Skylon told me more than once that Dorien's bravado was often an act. He was expected to be his father's son – confident, charming, at ease with men and women but in truth found it difficult to curb his passions, often becoming reckless but he was, at heart a decent man and would make a good and fair ruler.

There are many things I learned that night. One, different men find different things entertaining and pleasurable, and it is important, as a courtesan, to figure out what those pleasures are. Two, one need not be in a room to watch what goes on within it, and that watching can be pleasurable in and of itself. And three, one need not be with another to learn what pleases them, or what pleases yourself.

I had been led upstairs to the top floor to an odd, circular room larger than most buildings I had heretofore had the opportunity to stay within. Wooden beds lined the walls covered with fluffy pillows and bedding. In the centre of the room a large circular table sat filled with food and drink, a single bench wrapped around the table providing seating. Above the table an oval floated, as tall as I was, and the only thing my mind could think of was "mirror", but somehow, I knew that it was not. It was not as luxurious as the guest rooms, but it beat the cramped caravans I was used to. This room appeared to be one of rest and relaxation for the girls and, I was surprised to see, some lads of my own age. I would learn soon enough that some of the 'concubines' provided specific services, some were rested, or healing and a few were initiates like myself. The initiates often acted as servants to the more experienced, learning more than just the skills of the bedchamber, and of course, we would study and refine ourselves.

Tatia entered the room the young women and handsome boys bowed in respect. "This is Celestine of the desert folk beyond the great volcanic ridge known as the Mountains of Fire. She is the Principal Concubine to his Serene Highness, the Prince of the Snowy Sky from the High Palace. She has one month to prepare herself for this honoured task. But." She paused dramatically as she eyed those within. "His Highness requires that none may touch her save for himself, which shall make teaching more interesting. We shall have a month of lessons in watching and reading and demonstrating."

She held two locks of hair, one bluish white and the other golden strawberry, tied with ribbons of gold. Placing them into a dish of abalone below the oval and slowly a library came into focus within its glow. "One can see and not be seen."

The youth gathered about the table began to sup. Treela led me to the table and we ate as we watched the pleasures of the two princes unfold beneath.

****

"There is a gentleman's game room down that hall if you do not wish to mingle with the guests in the parlour; and a library, where you may choose to peruse the available reading materials. I'm sure you'll find something...enlightening there. The only rules are that you do not go upstairs unless you have been invited, and the word 'stop' always means stop. Now, please, make yourselves at home. I'll send someone along to fetch you a tray of refreshments in a few moments"

"I am unused to taking orders from women," Dorien mumbled to his brother. "I am used to giving them."

Her laugh rose around them, "Then young lord, you have a great deal to learn. A man must yield as well as conquer. And you, Skylon, does this place displease you?"

Skylon gazed around the library and found it did not. He was curious, besides he enjoyed watching his brother squirm. They had got into much strife with their father for the escapade with the caravan, and it had taken much persuasion to placate him. Skylon had realised this was a punishment as well as an education. Dorien had not. "No, a man must learn to be prepared for all eventualities. My brother is headstrong and can be arrogant. A woman may lead as well as a man."

Dorien snorted and found Tatia's grip on his chin strong and firm. "Your brother is wiser than thee. You are in my care, and in this place, it means you are mine to do with as I please. I can assure you when you leave you will thank me and you will remember all your lives what is taught in these halls. Passion may be tamed or wild and may control or be controlled, whether that is a passion for a woman, for war, or for gold. Would you be a slave to them? You are noble men, tis true but so are all who come here."

She snapped her fingers and an entertainer came down the stairs. Short blond ringlets pulled up into pony-tails on either side of her head and bright amber eyes, which sparkled as she curtsied before the brothers. The short white gown that fluffed into layers of ruffles at her hips, ended well above her knees and her legs were long and upon her face was a white feather mask. "Felicity, the young men need a guide. I will arrange for refreshments."

As the brothers walked down the hall indicated by Tatia's pointed finger, she whispered into Felicity's ear, "The pale one, Skylon, his is a gentle soul. He needs...careful cultivation. I leave him in your tender hands."

"And the other?"

"I'll send someone for him," Tatia smiled.

The library seemed small compared to their own back at the High Palace but appeared well stocked. A grand fireplace filled one wall made of black stone. Above it a cameo carving in white and grey of men and women in a variety of erotic poses. A window framed either side of the fireplace, blood red curtains casting a glow over a room panelled in rich, honeyed wood. The room was easily half again as tall, with a thin black iron balcony circling the room from a thin spiral stairway beside the door.

The few reading tables in the room were scattered with open books. Dorien wandered past the stacks, dragging his hand along the spines of the volumes as Skylon sat at one of the tables, slowly flipping through the book before him. He craned forward, wrapping his arms around the book as he read.

Shaking his head Dorien threw himself down into one of the dark leather chairs, draping his leg casually over the arm. "Father brings us to a... gentlemen's club, and we're sent to the library to study," Dorien sighed in exasperation.

Skylon replied without looking up from the book he had found, "Oh, I think even you could find something in here that you would consent to study, if only you would open a book or two."

"Bah," Dorien snorted, "I'll leave the studying to you. I prefer to be doing something."

A serving girl entered the library carrying a silver tray filled with fruits and sweets. Setting the tray upon a table, the woman curtseyed and held out a small pair of silver scissors. Felicity took the scissors and approached the young Princes. "If you please, a small token is required to show that you are being served. Just a lock of hair to be bound in gold."

With a shrug, the lads nodded and Felicity carefully snipped a lock from each, tied them with a golden ribbon, and returned them to the serving girl with the scissors. Another young woman entered the library as the serving girl left and quietly crossed the room.

Curtseying to the young men, she lifted a book from the case in the wall across from the fireplace. With a soft click, the case swung open to reveal a hidden room. "I am Lei," she smiled as she bowed low before Dorien. Her skin shimmered from some sweet-smelling powder that tried to pale her olive complexion. He took her hand and kissed it softly, never taking his eyes away from her dark almond-shaped eyes that called to him. Now, this was more like it!

"Come, we shall offer you refreshment in the gentlemen's lounge. Madam does not like liquids spilt near her books."

Panelled in red mahogany, the room was definitely a place for men. Thick, heavy black wood furniture, deep, comfortable leather chairs, a large wooden bar stocked with spirits and wine, a sturdy barrel of ale, card table, chess table, and some odd large rectangular table covered in green soft cloth. Felicity set the tray on a serving table with a smile, "What may I get you, gentlemen?"

Choosing a chair beneath a bright light, Skylon opened his book, "I'm content to read, thank you."

"And you found nothing to your liking in the library, young master?" Lei asked Dorien as she filled a tankard of ale for him.

He took the ale and drank deeply, pausing to press the back of his hand to his mouth as he swallowed. "A fine ale," he rasped, trying not to cough. At home, they always had watered ale, and he was sure this was a good deal stronger than even cook's usual brew. Wine and mead were more the fare he was used to. Ale was generally not served to the nobility, who thought themselves above such things. The taste was not unpleasant, but it was unfamiliar.

Taking the cup from his hand, Lei set it on the table, "Come now, let me show you a few things that I think you might like." She trailed her finger under his chin as she stepped towards the library door, winking at Felicity as she passed.

****

Felicity propped on the arm of the chair and bent over resting her cheek on the top of Skylon's head. "What are you reading?"

"Uh," he said as he turned the book over to look at the spine. "The Budding Lotus," he replied absently before turning the book around and beginning to read again.

"Read it to me," she whispered as she placed her hand on his chest.

"Hmm?" he replied without looking up.

She could feel his breath was fast as he read, so she whispered again, "Read to me."

His voice was soft and warm, reminding her of the breeze through a summer meadow she had felt once on one of her few trips outside the Painted Lady. She rested there, her cheek atop his head, her hand gently caressing his chest as he read, little by little opening the buttons on his shirt, gathering no notice from him at all.

Lei started up the thin spiral stairway that led to the balcony above. As Dorien started up after her, he whistled long and low when he noticed she wore not a thing below her crimson ruffled short gown. She paused at the top, bending over just slightly as though looking at a book on a lower shelf. Slowing in his ascent, he stopped just short of touching her, and she leaned to one side, looking up at him from behind her own legs, "Have you seen anything that interests you yet, young master?"

Reaching out his hand slowly, he trailed it down her thigh before taking the railing beside her and stepping up, gently brushing against her exposed skin, "I might have, but you were going to show me something?"

"Ah, yes," she smiled as she stood up. She reached up to a high shelf, stretching on her tiptoes before pulling down a well-worn tome, turning towards him as she regained her footing. Her tunic was untied and pushed down into the top of her bodice, leaving her perky breasts exposed, her caramel nipples brushing against his chest as she stumbled forward.

He backed down the stairs slowly, looking up at her the entire way, stumbling as he missed the last step. She caught him by the collar of his shirt and pulled him into a soft kiss, the old tome squeezed between them. "We should return to the lounge," she whispered in his ear before pushing him back a few steps.

Heart racing, Dorien ran his fingers through his golden-strawberry waves and sucked in a deep breath as he watched her pause at the door, motioning him forward with one finger. Exhaling loudly, he returned to the lounge, hardly noticing as the hidden door swung closed behind him.

Lei led him to the card table where she pointed to the chair. Setting the book on the table, she fetched his ale and then settled into his lap, wiggling just a bit. Feeling him hard against her backside, she smiled as she slid back and forth just a little. He squeezed her waist and groaned into her ear, "Oh no, I know where that is going, and it doesn't interest me at all. I've no interest in being wiggled on until I wet my breeches as my brother has done. I want proper entertainments."

Opening the book, she began to flip the pages, "Do you see anything here that interests you, perhaps?" Each page of the book held a different illustration of people in erotic poses. Men, women, sometimes several of each, all offering pleasure. Slipping both hands beneath her skirt he began to rub her, inhaling deeply as his fingers entered her warmth and she pushed against him.

Rubbing her pip with his thumb he held her firmly to his hips, "You're going to have to do better than that."

She leant back against his chest, tipping her head back until she could kiss along his jaw. Spreading her legs wide she pulled one of his hands to her breasts as his fingers played in her wetness. She bit his neck just below his ear and he hissed through his teeth."If you want to study the knowledge of this tome, then I have somewhere I can take you...if you ask nicely."

"Yes," he breathed desperately.

"That is not asking nicely," she teased as she tried to stand up.

He pulled her back into his lap, kissing her forcefully. He pointed to the open page of the book, "That one...please show me."

"Ambitious," she replied with a giggle as she slid from his lap, scooping up the book. Crossing the room, she pressed a silver ornament on the wall, a panel sliding open to reveal another hidden doorway, and another iron spiral staircase climbing into the dark.

"Skylon," Dorien called, but Lei placed her fingers over his mouth, shushing him.

"This journey is for you to take with me. I do not believe he is yet ready for the secrets this book contains." Dorien nodded and followed her up the stairs towards a warm, pink light above, the panel sliding closed behind them.

****

Skylon had watched as Dorien left and returned, pausing only briefly as he read, the girl resting gently at his elbow. He sighed as she rubbed his chest but tried hard to concentrate on the words. Dorien had done nothing but tease him about his "accident" since their visit with the dancing girls. Always the more athletic of the two, Skylon wondered if his brother had found yet another sport to excel in as he watched Dorien follow Lei up the hidden staircase.

Felicity stroked Skylon's cheek and kissed him softly, "Did you want to go with them?"

"No," he shook his head decisively. "I think he'll enjoy himself more without me."

She kissed him again, sliding from the arm of the chair, "Read from page three hundred."

"What?" he asked, confused.

"Page three hundred," she said, trailing her fingers along his cheek as she circled behind the chair.

Flipping through the book he began to read aloud, "The bud lay unopened, soft and inviting. The kiss of the morning sun warmed it. The breath of the spring breeze tickled it. Slowly the petals began to unfurl."

He looked over the top of the book to see Felicity before him. She opened the hooks on the front of her bodice one by one as he read, dropping it to the floor beneath her feet. Absently he rubbed his throat, only then realising his shirt was already unbuttoned.

Clearing his throat, he read further, "The flower opens, turning to face the sun, basking in the glow as the rays warm every petal and not just the outside leaves."

Glancing up he swallowed as she unlaced the top of her short gown letting is slowly slide down her body to pool at her feet. Her skin was creamy white, every inch, save for her nipples and her womanhood, which were rosy pink. He coughed, reaching to the table beside him seeking a drink, but touching empty wood, continued to read, "The gentle butterfly lands upon the flower, drinking deeply of her nectar with his long tongue, probing deeply to reach her sweetness."

The clink of glass on wood startled him, and he looked over to see a pint of ale at his side. Picking it up he downed half quickly before having a chance to realise how strong it was. He took in a deep breath and held it, letting it out slowly. He watched as Felicity lay across a low, cushioned bench nearby, one arm draped over her head as the other stroked her stomach, legs bent at the knees as her body flowed over the bench.

Taking another deep swallow of ale, he picked the book up again, "As night falls the petals close around the swollen fruit, hugging it close. A gentle breeze blows, rocking the flower back and forth as the fruit rides inside. A gentle rain begins to fall, spattering its warmth across the petals, the breeze stirring them like fingers, spreading the drops over themselves as they sigh at the touch."

The book slid from his hands to the floor as he watched the girl draw her fingers across her belly. He swallowed the last of his ale as he stood, carefully placing the cup on the table before crossing to where she lay. Closing his eyes, he knelt at the end of the bench and bent over her, resting his cheek against her belly while she stroked his hair. He inhaled deeply and whispered something she could not hear before kissing her softly on her warm womanhood.

****

Dorien stepped into a large, round chamber, walls covered in creamy silk, red scarves hanging from brass rings about the circle, giant rosette window of reds and golds shining down on a long oval-shaped bed draped in a soft, plush cloth such as he had never felt. He watched as the panel slid home behind them, completely blending into the wall, matching every other panel that had no scarf upon it.

Lei circled the room, dragging her hand along the wall, scarves swinging as they flipped over her hand. She stopped at an empty panel and pulled a golden tassel that hung from the golden wood strip that divided the panels. She walked towards him, slowly unfastening her bodice. As he stepped towards her, she raised a finger, wiggling it at him, "Ah, ah, ah...you have chosen a pleasure, young master, and you shall receive it. But that pleasure is for us to provide to you. We are your servants, but you are not to lift a finger. You are here to receive. When we are done, you may choose again."

The panel beside the gold tassel slid open and a forest elf from the lands beyond the seas stepped through. Long, wavy chestnut hair framed a delicate face and long ears, eyes the colour of a forest pool beheld him; she wore a golden bodice that lifted her breasts and hugged her tiny waist. Her quim was clean-shaven with a silver ring through the area just above her womanhood, a dainty pearl riding just upon her pip. She stalked past him, dragging her fingers across his chest as she bent over, flipping the cover up on the bed.

She reached beneath and several clicks could be heard. With a gentle shove, the round ends swung away leaving a narrow-cushioned bench in the centre. The woman watched his chest rise and fall, nearly panting as though he had run a race. She undressed him with agonising slowness, one button at the time, tugging the tail of his shirt from his trousers bit by bit, sliding the shirt down his arms, hands caressing the taut muscles, her nipples peeking over the top of her bodice teasing his chest.

Grabbing the waist of his pants, she pulled him along as she walked backwards, stopping when she reached the bench. She knelt before him, taking his boots and tossing them aside before reaching up to unfasten his belt and slide his pants to the floor. A soft whisper in his ear commanded him, "Lay upon the bench and relax. You will find handholds below it if you need them to help you...keep your hands to yourself. Remember, you are not to lift a finger."

Lei walked around to stand beside the bench, and Dorien turned, compelled to do her bidding. She pointed to the bench, smirking as he sat on the end and looked between the two of them. Lei snapped and the elven girl in gold bowed her head and walked around the open wing of the bed to stand at the other end of the bench. "Lay back young master, she waits for you."

The girl pulled at the end of the bench and a small shelf slipped out, angled down slightly. Dorien grinned broadly and lay back, scooting himself until his head lay just at the proper angle to pleasure the girl. He reached for her, and Lei slapped his hand, "Hands, young master, or I may be forced to bind you."

He lifted an eyebrow but felt under the bench and discovered smooth poles running the length of the bench. He grabbed hold as he tilted his head back. The commanding tone she used was a novelty. No one save his father and mother dared order the Prince of the Rosy Dawn. Coming from the painted lips of this sultry woman he found it incredibly alluring. The girl stepped forward, her pearl hovering over his lips. Leaning forward she placed her hands on his chest and moaned as his tongue slowly passed over her, circling around, but not yet entering, the tip finding the silver ring and flicking it as she gasped.

Lei nodded, walking along the bench trailing her nails down his chest, over his abdomen, and across his thigh. Reaching the end of the bench she pushed his legs open wide as she softly stroked both his thighs while exhaling hot breath over his member. Sliding her fingers under his hips, she pressed up with her nails as she took him fully into her mouth in one hot pass, curling her tongue around him as she slowly drew back up.

Dorien moaned, arms clenched as he pulled against the grips under the bench. The girl atop him was so sweet, and Lei's long deep strokes made his blood boil. His mouth worked her, licking and sucking, and he learned that pulling the ring caused her to gasp and wiggle. As Lei pumped him slowly, sucking deeply, urging his hunger on.

Wanting to drink deeply from the girl, he reached out and grabbed her, pulling her down until he could plunge his tongue into her. His fingers pressed into her buttocks and she groaned, rubbing herself over his face. He gasped as the sensitive skin of his inner thigh was bitten, and then those nails began their tickling dance up his body.

Lei walked around the walls, grabbing a scarf as she moved, stopping behind the elf girl. She spanked her hard, the sound of slapped skin echoing about the room. "No hands," she repeated. She took his hands and bound them at the wrists, then spanked the girl again. "Pleasure him."

The girl crawled down his chest, nipples teasing him as their rosy peaks brushed down his body. She wrapped one hand around the base of his manhood as she took it slowly into her mouth. He inhaled deeply, a fast, hissing sound as something tantalised him, sensitive from Lei's previous attentions.

A hot voice whispered in his ear as she pulled his arms back behind his head and tied them below the shelf, "She has a...special toy...it is pierced through her tongue, and many a man finds it drives them insane. She is specially trained and can place pressure exactly where it is needed to hold you there, at the edge of release, until you beg her to let you go. The girls in gold are here to serve you, to meet your every need, so long as you do not touch them. If you use your hands, you will be bound until you reach release."

She kissed him deeply, passionately, and his hunger stirred again. "You chose a picture of two women seeking pleasure with a man, and so you shall have it."

She raised the shelf so that his head was tilted up towards his chest, as though propped on cushions. She climbed up to sit on his chest, propping a foot on each of the open wings of the bed. He groaned as the elf girl pumped him faster and faster as Lei slid towards him. He kissed her once but could feel his peak building. His biceps bulged as he pulled against the binding, crying out as he crested with his mouth to her cleft.

The girls slid from him, each taking a wing of the bed and folding it back, gently lifting his legs as they latched everything back together. Lei pulled the fluffy blanket over him and untied his wrists. "You may stay here until your father returns, choosing your pleasures, or you may return to the Madam's suites, the choice is yours. I am to be your escort as long as you have need of me."

****

Felicity's legs curled tighter around Skylon's back, her knees over his shoulders as he pleasured her, his arms wrapped around her thighs. She arched her back, reaching down to run her fingers through his long pale hair. Touching her only with his mouth, he stroked her until her sighs became moans and her hands clenched in his hair. Her legs pressed against his face, toes pointed, as she lifted her hips to meet him more fully, her moans becoming cries as she reached her peak.

Releasing her, he sat back as her legs slid from his shoulders, shudders shaking her as she lay on the bench before him. He crawled across the floor and retrieved her short gown, bringing it to her as he sat on the floor beside her. She sat up and looked at him quizzically, "Did you not want more, young master?"

"No," he said as he crossed his arms in front of his knees.

She pulled the gown over her head, tying the drawstring at the neckline, "Am I not pleasing to you, young master?"

"No," he whispered, "Yes...I mean, you are lovely. It's just that..."

She smiled and patted his arm, "What if we visit the kitchens, see about a proper bit of food and drink. Then I'll show you to your room."

Skylon looked over to the panel, "What about Dorien?"

"He is for Lei to attend to. Would you like to bring the book, or perhaps choose another?"

"Maybe I'll come back later to choose another. I think I've learned what I needed to from this one."

                                   ✳✳✳✳

Skylon lay on his side in a dreamy half-sleep, soft breath at the back of his neck and delicate arm wrapped around his waist. His mind drifted back to nights in the nursery when he and Dorien shared a bed. Sons of the Principal Wife and concubine, born on the same night during a frigid blizzard, one had been welcomed by snowfall and the other had ushered in the dawn as the storm passed.

They had always shared a bed, as far back as he could remember, raised as twins though one would become High King and the other was destined as consort to the Goddess. They had moved to a suite of their own a few years ago, just down the hall from their father's chambers which led to his Zenana. Skylon often missed the close camaraderie of the Zenana, for once they had been outgrown the nursery, they stopped having siblings other than one another, and even the youthful servants they had been raised alongside in the nursery would no longer look them in the eye when addressed.

Sighing as his memory wandered, he turned in his bed, startled at finding warm skin as his hand reached out. His eyes popped open and he saw a slim figure, skin of soft caramel hue, curled beside him. She wore nothing save a white veiled hood which completely covered her head, wrapping her hair and hiding her face above her nose.

"Who are you?" he asked as she pulled his hand to lay on her stomach.

"Who do you need me to be?" she whispered as she rolled towards him, sliding her hand up his chest as his caressed her back.

"I don't understand." He shook his head as she straddled him, nothing between her warmth and his manhood save the thin linen of his nightshirt.

The woman bowed over him, trailing her lips over his throat, along his jaw, to his ear, "Close your eyes," her warm breath teased. Soft fingers covered his mouth, "Shhh, don't talk, just feel."

He did as bid and settled back into his pillow, breathing uneasily, tense all over. He jumped at every touch but did go so far as to pull away. She smiled, exhaling in a soft laugh, hardly perceptible as she rolled partially atop him, fingers of one hand entwining with his as the other stroked his cheek. "Don't think...relax...let go..."

With every stroke of her fingers across his cheek, he felt calmer, lighter, as though drifting into a comfortable sleep. As he relaxed, she continued to caress him over his nightshirt, softly kissing his face until he sighed long and deep. Laying fully atop him she entwined the fingers of her other hand into his as she continued kissing his face and neck, softly exhaling into his ears. She began to move her hips against his over his nightshirt, smiling softly as his body responded to hers.

He returned her kisses, softly at first, slowly yielding to her gentle prodding, letting her tongue play with his, passion building slowly like clouds rolling in over the mountains to drizzle refreshing rain over the valley. She led him in this slow dance, pulling him along, but never pushing, until finally he released her hands and slid his arms around her back to embrace her. As she rubbed over him, his nightshirt moved with her, slowly rolling up until his skin met hers.

He moaned as her wetness moved over him, warm and inviting. His hands travelled up her back and framed her face as he kissed her deeply. Fingers slipped under the veil, but her hands pulled him away. Entwining her fingers with his, she pressed his hands into the pillow above his head as she slowly pushed herself onto his member.

Sucking his breath between his teeth as he tilted his head back. She was warm and wet, and it felt very tight, sheathing his cock like a glove. Skylon moaned, the cry escaping his lips as her muscles squeezed. She panted into his shoulder, gasping, almost whining as she forced herself, her nails digging into the back of his hands. Long slow strokes, completely different from the dancing girl who had gyrated atop him at the festival, worked him. And the pleasure built.

Instead of hurried and frantic, this was slow and soft. Instead of hungry and demanding, this was gentle and giving. They moved together as one, holding hands, her breath warm on his neck sending shivers down his spine. He built slowly, cresting with a soft moan as he slid into warmth, like settling into a bath. She kissed him deeply before rolling away.

Dorien crossed the room from the chair where he had been sitting, quietly observing and unseen. Propping on the edge of the bed beside the girl he placed his hand over her womanhood and concentrated, gently warming her with a healing spell. She began to pant, curling around his hand as she held on to his arm. She moaned as he channelled more power into the spell while he grasped the back of her neck and pulled her over into a passionate kiss. She cried out just as his hand began to tingle and he fell to one knee beside the bed.

"That was amazing," she whispered.

"I know," he grinned before kissing her again.

Skylon leant on one elbow as he watched, "How did you learn to do that?"

"I have learned many things while you slept, some of which actually came from books, believe it or not. Come, I have things to show you, and your room needs tending now."

He kissed the girl again and trailed a finger beneath her chin, "What colour will you wear now?"

"Gold, young master."

"Then we will see you in Lei's chambers when you have cleaned up." She bowed her head as he left.

Reaching out she took Skylon's arm as he stood from the bed, "Remember that it can be gentle when you lie with the one whose face you see behind your closed eyes. She waits for you."

Skylon caught up to Dorien who waited for him in a lounge in the Madam's parlour, "Why did you ask her about the colour she wears?"

"Have you not learned anything since you've been here? No, I doubt you did more than read until just now. The white signified she was pure, but now that you have opened the blossom, she'll move on to a new colour. Come on; you're not going to lay about in bed all day, are you?"

****

That month I spent at the Painted Lady was the most exciting, and educational, of my life up until then. I read; I watched; I learned, and in the end, I was pleased that it had been the Prince of the Snowy Sky who had chosen me. He was soft and gentle and as interested in learning about me as he was in telling me about himself and his life. His brother, on the other hand, seemed to burn with a fire within, seeking out every new experience the Painted Lady had to offer.

Although we had spent much of our time together, the Prince of the Snowy Sky had never once touched me other than in friendly ways. The day before we were set to part, we sat out in the walled courtyard garden on a long, wooden bench swing. He was reading to me from a book of poetic verses when his brother lifted my feet, slid beneath them, and joined us on the bench.

Skylon lounged on the bench swing in the warmth of the morning sun, one leg outstretched across it, the other foot dangling, toe slowly swaying the bench as it rested in the grass. Celestine snuggled against his chest, head on his shoulder, legs stretched out alongside his, eyes closed as she listened to him read. She sighed as his arm slid around her waist, his head leaning back against the rope at the corner of the bench as he balanced the book in one hand on the back of the swing.

She was startled from her dreamy state by her legs being lifted from their rest. She opened her eyes to see Dorien squeezing in on the end of the bench. Skylon bent his knee to give his brother more room as Dorien reached over and took the book. He flipped through, trailing his fingers down the pages. Smiling brightly, he handed the book back to Skylon.

Clearing his throat, Skylon began to read in a soft voice, "The majestic bird preened his emerald feathers until he glistened like a jewel in the summer sun. Standing in the shadows, hidden, unnoticed, the bird of grey watched as the jewel strutted past, seemingly unknowing, unseeing."

Dorien lay his hand on Celestine's thigh, softly caressing as Skylon continued to read, "She followed along, ever nearby, ever watching, always waiting; but when he turned to look for the soul he felt calling to him, all he saw was the shades of grey in his shadow."

Leaning towards her, Dorien placed his hand over hers, sliding her hand over Skylon's. The three wove their fingers together as Skylon continued to read, "The jewel waited in the sun, sparkling, brilliant, and alone. He hung his head as the clouds began to form."

Dorien slid his hand away, leaving the fingers of the others still entwined. He drew his fingers slowly over her dress, tickling her womanhood as he stroked down her inner thigh and back up again long, soft gentle strokes. She closed her eyes and sighed, tilting her head back, forehead nearly at Skylon's chin.

Breathing deeply, Skylon's voice grew softer, "The grey of the day merged with the shadows, and the majestic one curled in the grass, head on her wing, waiting for the coming rain. The shadow moved, creeping ever closer, spreading her wings as the first drops began to fall." Placing his hand above theirs, he gently slid them over Celestine's gown until they rested above her womanhood.

Skylon hesitated, voice faltering as Dorien rubbed their fingers over Celestine's warmth below her thin spring gown. Dorien squeezed Skylon's arm and he continued, "The chill wind blew and he looked up to see her shivering. He stood, spreading his fan, shielding her from the winds. Shelter one for the other, no longer alone, their colours merge as they come together as one."

Dorien slid from the bench, lifting the book from Skylon's hand as he stood, smiling as his brother continued to gently stroke Celestine through the gown. Weaving an arm behind Skylon's neck, she pulled up to kiss him deeply as Dorien walked away through the garden.

The High City

The journey from the festival to the capital had been long and lazy, and it was difficult for me to guess how far we had come, which was quite unusual considering I had spent my entire life up until this point as a nomad in a caravan. Generally, I was quite good with tracking direction and distance, so I attributed this discrepancy to being in a new land and frequent stops to visit some important location or another along our journey.

When we first arrived outside the great city, I simply stared in amazement, for never in all my travels had I seen such a place. It looked very nearly like a sea of city, if such a thing is even possible, flowing over the landscape like rolling waves, a veritable rainbow of brightly coloured buildings. I could only imagine the number of people within would be like the oceans of fish darting to and fro on their daily journeys.

Beside the city lay the great circle of a harbour, half again as large as the city itself, the natural spits of land to either side elongated by sea walls such that only one ship at the time could pass through. In the distance a lone hill could be seen, a white ribbon snaking its way back and forth across the face. Atop the hill shimmered in the sunlight as though a great mirror sat upon the height reflecting the sun.

At the city's edge, we changed carriages, from the covered hulks of long travel to decorative, open-topped touring coaches.

The Prince of the Rosy Dawn rode in the first coach with Treela, Felicity, and Lei from the Painted Lady. I rode in the second coach with the Prince of the Snowy Sky. The carriages and wagons of our retinue diverged from our path, and the Prince explained they would take a less conspicuous route to the palace.

We trailed through the city accompanied by much fanfare; musicians, dancers, children throwing flowers, ladies in windows craned out bare-breasted and tossed tokens, some of which were retrieved by fleet footmen at a signal from the Prince of Dawn, who seemed to revel in the attentions. The Prince of the Sky merely sat, and waved, nodding and smiling, holding my hand in his lap as we rode. A few times he leant into me, brushing his nose over my cheek or sniffing my hair, and on occasion, we spoke softly as he patiently answered my questions.

The girls from the Painted Lady would be Dorien's first courtesans. He had asked for Treela to be his Principal Concubine, but their father had refused the pairing saying that no child born of the Earth Clan would be able to serve as Consort to the Goddess, should a new Consort be required. In truth, Dorien had wanted Treela as his bride, but his Principal Wife had been named for him at her birth, oldest daughter of a noble house which travelled to a faraway land to establish a new colony.

As the young lady had been escorted to the palace when she came of age, there was not much Dorien could do about the arrangement, but he planned to meet with his mother for her intercessions to have Treela raised to secondary wife. His mother was, in fact, the daughter of a forest elf, which was why Dorien's colouration was darker than others, and he was certain she would aid him.

Skylon carefully explained the traditions to me, how the oldest son of the High King's Principal Wife would always be the next heir, and the oldest son of the Principal Concubine would always be held aside for the Goddess. The current consort was already quite elderly, so while Skylon expected to be called to the Temple, he did not think Dorien's son would ever be called.

He also explained how ladies travelled from all over the Sky Kingdom, and often from beyond, in the hopes of one night at the Palace. The tokens were inscribed with the lady's name and might be redeemed by any male of the royal family for one night. For one year, she would live in the city and want for nothing, and if a child was born, she would sometimes move to the Zenana as a courtesan. For many, it was a coveted opportunity. The family of the young lady would receive honour, and if she were particularly fecund, would receive titles. I was told many of the noble houses here began as the bastard offspring of one prince or another. Girl-children would train as diplomats, ladies of the bedchamber, or sometimes consorts to distant allies as Skylon's mother had, being a highborn from beyond the Great Lake settlements. Boys would train in arms, or if particularly favoured, manage one of the outer holdings as lord.

Did my prince have a Principal Wife appointed to him as well? No, he had said, marriage was not his lot in life. When the time came, he would be Consort to the Goddess herself at the Temple of the Sky. Until that time, he could take concubines as it pleased him, but his children would never do more than serve a temple. And as for courtesans, the temples had well enough of those. He felt no need to gather more. Unlike his brother and father, his blood did not run so hot.

Eventually, we arrived at the base of the hill where a litter bedecked with cloth-of-gold waited to carry us. The narrow road snaked back and forth in twisting turns up the face of the hill, framed by high walls. As we settled in the litter, Lei looked about and asked, "But where are the footmen?"

With a chuckle, the Prince of Dawn shook his head and replied, "We have no need for footmen here, for this is hallowed ground, and the Goddess hears her children. Skylon?"

Skylon grinned – more confident on his own ground. "Home!" he commanded and the litter lifted from the ground and began to fly. I grabbed the edge, my stomach flipping as we glided onward. Dorien chuckled at my greenish look and wide eyes, "It surprises everyone that way, but one gets used to it. Skylon has more power than I here, at least when such skills are required."

I nodded unconvinced, but my clenched hand did not dare leave the edge or Skylon's own and he winced slightly as my frightened fingers dug in. "I think she prefers her feet on solid ground, brother, or someone's feet anyway."

Lei caught my eye, "I'll never get used to this. It's not right." She too looked uneasy.

"You'll not say that when I take my pleasures with you in a similar craft. The soft rocking motion enhancing your delight, and the warm breeze on that shapely backside will cause you to think more highly of such a vehicle." Dorien ran his finger around her breast and nipped at her ear.

"Do you ever think of anything else?" His brother asked, rolling his eyes.

"Why should I, when I have the pick of women here? I am a man of passion. There will be time for boring state-craft and thoughts of duty when Father is gone. Until then I intend to enjoy myself."

****

The crowning jewel of the Sky Kingdom was truly that, the vast expanse of a jewelled palace, gardens, and the great temple to the Goddess of the Sky sitting high atop the hill overlooking the sprawling city below. From the seat of the litter, I could see women, children, and youth wandering towards the hedge, but none stepped beneath the archway to greet us. Beyond them, I could see tall hedges and fortified stone walls, gateways, fountains, statues and columns, and sprinkles of colours from plants I could not identify. I released my jaw had dropped open in wonder at such a sight. Never in all my days, which I admit were fewer then, had I seen such a glorious place. There was no question of who held the reins of power here. Here and there, atop the walls, bobbed a helmed and plumed head of a palace soldier, and I spotted unfamiliar devices which I later learned were siege-engines. There had been little call to use them in the present king's lifetime but life in the Sky Kindom had not always been so peaceful.

The doors of the palace opened and a petite woman with auburn hair, freckled skin, and sparkling green eyes stepped forward and waited demurely, yet serenely. Extending her arms, she smiled as the Prince of Dawn stepped forward, and I saw him bow his head to her. I'd never seen him give obsequience to any save his father.

"Welcome home, my son! I see that you waste no time in filling your hall and gathering tokens." She dropped the tokens one by one into his hand and smiled, "Your father has claimed his tax already. Come, a bath has been prepared; then we shall dine."

With that, we were led, wide-eyed, gaping-mouthed, and breathless through the palace to a grand suite of rooms where a young woman of the elves waited. I noted a few female faces peeking from behind pillars and curtains and silent guards whose eyes were kept firmly ahead of them. Skylon later told me these men were either eunuchs or known to prefer their own sex. No man of regular tastes would be allowed within these walls unescorted, except the High King and his sons. Such was punishable by public execution. In my less worldly days, I'd asked what manner of man a eunuch might be and been shocked at the answer. In my later days, I'd employed such individuals as a guard, or spy or entertainer.

"My lord husband." She paused and eyed the group that entered, obviously displeased and taken by surprise. Her gown was flowing gown of red and orange, the layers of colours almost giving the impression of firelight. It was a becoming outfit, and as I was later to learn reflected her fiery will and nature. As with many of her kind delicate features held within a proud spirit. I would later feel some pity for this woman, but now I just avoided her glare.

The Prince of Dawn's mother stepped in front of us and nodded to the young lady, who stepped back and continued to glower. "I am Lady Kyra, Principal Wife of his most Exalted Highness, King of the Sky Realm and all it surveys. I am the First amongst all ladies of the household and all which concerns them. You will refer to me as Madam First, or Principal Lady and you will obey my commands. I do not care for disorder or squabbling. Nor do I condone spitefulness.

"Welcome to your new home, for this is the Zenana, the hall of women, for the Prince of Dawn. You have full access to this hall, and the gardens without, and the women's quarters as long as there is no locked gate. From this moment on, you will never leave either without your prince."

Placing her hand on the quiet young woman's back, gently Lady Kyra pushed her forward. "This is Lady Antheia, Principal Wife to the Prince of Dawn, and head of his personal Zenana. She will help you learn the expectations of life at court and arrange for lessons in any skills that need cultivating. I understand there are those with magic to be properly trained."

She clapped her hands, and several matrons appeared from behind a curtain at the end of the room. "Dorien, your suite is there, to the right. It also has an exit into the hall for when you entertain guests who are not of your harem. Tonight, you will escort Antheia to dine with us. You'll provider her with entertainment and care for three nights at least before I will release these tokens."

The Prince of Dawn had eyed his mother but then shrugged and walked off through the curtain at the end of the room, quickly followed by one of the matrons. Lady Kyra then turned to the Prince of Sky.

"Skylon, I did not wish for your concubine to become lonely, so you have a connecting suite here as well until you need a Zenana for yourself before you are called to temple work. But you must go and pay your respects to the High Priestess soon, decorum and duty demand it. Now, if you would be so kind, escort the ladies to the bath. This hall is exactly as the one you grew up in."

Skylon bowed to the two ladies and kissed each on the hand before leading us through the curtain. We followed a long decorated hall with many doors down either side. At the far end, double doors opened onto an amazing site. In the centre of the floor was a pool, for surely it was the size of a small oasis, and the steam rose from it as though it were heated. Fountains of water rolled down the walls in some places, filling large clamshells to overflowing, running along patterned streams carved into the floor and into the pool. How this was achieved I knew not but could not wait to try it. During my days with the caravan, we bathed in rivers and ponds, or lugged buckets of heated water to a small sitting-tub or barrel. Usually, by the time it was my turn the water within was neither especially warm nor clean.

One entire wall of this great room was missing, open to the colourful garden beyond. And I learned later there was a hidden gallery for those who wished to view the bathers. Songbirds in golden cages sang to the sunset, and the air was both fragrant and tuneful. The matrons sat on a bench just inside near shelves of herbs and flowers, spices and perfumes, and prepared scented pouches for bathing as we each oohed and ahhed over the lavish items available. There were even lotions and oils and powders for after the bath to soften skin and hair.

Dorien stood naked in the warm water of the pool, a matron behind him combing scented oils through his hair. When he saw Skylon enter the bathhouse leading the girls, he smiled brightly, waved enthusiastically, "Come on, the water is wonderful. Dump those dirty travelling clothes and come pick out the scent you would like."

One by one the matrons undressed us and handed us the little pouches and sent us off towards the water where the princes were already bathing.

Dorien shooed his old nursemaid away. "Begone, Nana. Treela will see to my needs. Go prepare my new suite for an evening of fun after Father's dinner is seen to."

"I'm certain you'll not be receiving the type of fun you're seeking anytime soon, my young master. Your lady wife was none too pleased to give up her comfortable suite for your brother and his new lady," his old nursemaid replied with a throaty chuckle.

"Gave up her suite, did she? How kind of her. Where will she be staying then, in one of the smaller rooms within the hall?" he asked without any real interest.

"Oh, she's moved to your suite, I'm afraid. I believe your mother was teasing you when she said she would hold your tokens in safe-keeping...or perhaps she is keeping them safe, for I'm certain your lady wife has little interest in entertaining."

"Bah!" he exclaimed as he splashed the water. "Or interests in...never mind, she'll learn. The sooner she's borne a son, the better. Run along and prepare the chamber as Antheia prefers it, and I will make changes as I see fit after dinner."

Treela slid behind Dorien as the matron waded away and began to rub his back with the soft lamb's wool bag. She squeezed warm water over his shoulders, inhaling deeply, the musky scent enticing her. Dipping the scented bag into the water, she wrapped her arms around his chest as she pressed her breasts into his back, slowly drawing the bag across his chest, her long nails scoring red streaks as they passed.

He moaned as one of her hands slipped below the water. Pressing her mouth to his ear, she blew gently before playfully tugging at his earlobe as her hands continued to excite him. Suddenly she bit him just below the ear at that soft spot she knew roused him, and his breath hissed as he inhaled through his teeth. She answered his hissing with a throaty, guttural sound that was almost a growl.

Turning quickly, Dorien grabbed a handful of Treela's hair and kissed her passionately. Tearing himself away from her lips, he uttered in a husky voice, "No marks for now, my sweet. I wouldn't want the focus to be on me at tonight's dinner. Let Skylon and his darling have the spotlight for our return banquet. After my mother's requirements, have been met and Antheia's pride has been served, then you may have your way with me. I'll be sure you have a chamber set for your...specific skills. Until then..."

He hefted Treela onto his hips and carried her to the side of the pool where he deposited her on the tiled edge. Spreading her legs wide, he buried his face in her warmth as she moaned softly.

Felicity and Lei seemed to take no notice of the two, giggling and chatting as they bathed one another. Lei softly circled Felicity's breasts with her lamb's wool as she leaned in to whisper in her partner's ear. The lamb's wool slowly disappeared beneath the waters as Lei wrapped her other arm behind Felicity's back, trailing kisses down her neck and around her throat. Felicity's eyes closed and her head tipped back, a soft moan escaping her lips as Lei pleasured her beneath the waters.

Skylon muttered something and shook his head. "Come on, let's leave them to their...entertainment."

"You do not wish to be served thus?" I asked, assuming Skylon would want his fill. I was nervous, although my time at the Painted Lady had been instructive, I was still rather naive in the ways of love. Wrapping a towel around his waist, Skylon smiled. "I do not wish to share the pleasures I seek with you before an audience. Dorien enjoys such a show and multiple players in his games. I prefer to keep your secrets all to myself."

He kissed my hand lightly as the bath attendant wrapped a soft towel around me. "Come, along. The matrons will prepare us for the dinner, then we can visit with my mother while we wait for the others to prepare themselves. Perhaps later I can taste your delights..." His fingers weaved beneath the towel, and he kissed me. I would have gladly pleasured him there but I was his to command and so, feeling the heat below and trying to ignore it I followed Skylon as bid.

****

Now, I'm sure there are some who wonder at the thought of four young women being disrobed and sent into the bath with two young men, but I say to you every culture, time, and place have their own acceptable behaviours and oddities, and none of us were 'blushing brides'. Growing up in a travelling caravan of dancing girls, my entire life had comprised of group activities and modesty was a concept we did not learn. For the girls growing up in the Painted Lady, I can only guess that their lives were very similar, but I digress. After the bath, we were to learn the first of many traditions usually held within a Zenana.

****

Braids adorned with silver beads and ribbons tumbled along my back; it had taken the attendants much time to prepare the correct oils and dressings. A sensuous hint of jasmine rose from the adornment. The primary attendant who was assigned to my needs was an almond-eyed silent girl with amber skin and short, straight black hair. As her hands worked the creamy lotion into my skin her breath increased as long, creamy fingers skimmed my breasts. At a look from one of the older women, the girl sighed and dusted my skin with a shimmering powder.

I was brought a wide translucent robe, similar to the wraps and costumes I wore in my former life. Used to dressing myself I discovered this fine cloth tricky to settle correctly. The attendant shook her head firmly as I fumbled with the over-long scarf-like garment and motioned to let her dress me. My breasts were captured in a tight, sling of the soft scarf, then the lengths of cloth crossed at my back, with one side in front and one behind in a complicated fold. The girl handed me a silver brocade under-bust corset and put my hands on it to hold firm, whilst she began to lace me in. At a hand signal, the matron took over, such matters required the attentions of a senior servant. The mute girl delicately ruffled the cloth into a fine and elegant fan across my bust. She seemed to me to possess extra arms and coax the filmy sheer fabric to her will as her hands moved back and forth as in a dance. As the corset tightened I gasped and tried to wriggle away but the matron just chuckled and said, "Hold still, we are not done yet. These garments can be daunting and complicated at first but you'll soon get used to the technique. My lord prince prefers this to any other style and he chose this himself for you."

The fluttery ruffle now hovered just over my nipples, obscuring what lay beneath but hinting at treasures therein. The longer end of the scarf, now remaining the matron fanned down my back, like the feathers of a bird. Finally, the girl ran her hands over the 'tail' and I felt it stiffen. To this day I have no idea how, but the effect was most pleasing as I gazed at my reflection in the looking glass.

"How breathe you, my lady?" the matron, as she stepped back to check the draping of the cloth.

I inhaled, not quite as deeply as she would like, "Well enough, although if you loosen it, I would be more comfortable."

The matron replied, "You will get used to the feel of it, and in time they will be able to tighten it further. When I was your age the High King of the Waning Moon could circle my waist with his hands. "Tomorrow you will be marked with your prince's symbols, painted, and adorned to denote your importance. This will be your daily wear from now on within the Zenana. You will have various decorative gowns for use when the Prince of the Snowy Sky escorts you, as well as tunics for use in the gardens. "The matron paused and then smiled kindly "I am told you are a sooth-sayer...that you read the stars by night. A good pairing for our prince. May you bear his fruit before he is called to serve the Goddess."

Skylon had arrived from a chamber I'd not even noticed, having been focused on the dressing. He stopped when he saw me, and his eyes sparkled. "The most beautiful girl I have seen. A star in the sky indeed." Another matron followed him, tutting, "Master, we've not finished yet. I know you want to see her...."

"Just a little lower around the flourish and a little higher around the legs. We don't want her falling over it."

"Yes, yes, my young prince. You grew up in a Zenana and haven't been outside its doors too often. I'm sure you can advise her yourself. I'm just your silly old nursemaid, wanting to be sure she's ready to present."

"Now, Nain," he chuckled as his matron tied the sash around his waist, "I'm sure we'll have plenty of time before any official presentations are made, and Dorien will have his first as Antheia is his Principal Wife and a promised bride. You worry too much, and I promise she'll not leave my side until she's properly marked."

With a nod, Nain kissed Skylon on the cheek and then clapped her hands. Pressing a spot on the wall, a panel slid back and she led the girls through. As soon as the panel was closed, Skylon began to loosen my corset, much to my relief.

"I am sorry about that. Nain comes from an older tradition in the Zenanas. My grandfather was very much into ornamentation. Bare, painted breasts, a clean-shaven lotus rouged a bright colour, and tiny, wasp waists. Luckily for my mother, Father just likes bare breasts and jewels. Although of course, I avert my eyes from hers. Such business as that is forbidden.

"From the looks of Antheia when we arrived, I have doubts that she and her ladies have been keeping with the traditional dress while this hall belonged to them alone, and I suspect Dorien will have something to say about that now that he will be spending more time here. I will speak with Nain about ensuring to your comfort when you are dressed. I don't see a need for you to sit about breathlessly awaiting my attentions." Skylon smiled warmly and winked.

"That doesn't leave much to the imagination, at the front," I said to him, wriggling a bit under the unfamiliar fabric.

"Of course not!" Skylon responded. "The intent is to gain my attentions each time I see you." He pulled me close and breathed in my scent. Soon his lips had found the hollow of my neck and the plunge of my outfit. "Later I plan to unwrap you slowly. Sadly, there is no time for such amusements now."

With a resigned sigh, he led me to the large armoire decorated with gold filigree scrollwork. Skylon opened the doors to reveal a host of long open front overcoat style gowns in various linens, all in patterned shades of grey, silver, and white.

He chose a gown of white satin with glittering silver long-tailed stars all over it. There were three silver buttons that closed the gown just enough to cover the corset hooks. The sleeves were snug from shoulder to elbow, where they opened to long, scarf-like drapes. Kneeling, Skylon slipped dainty silver shoes upon my feet. "You look like the Stargazer your name suggests. None of Dorien's women are as fine or have such an unusual colouring."

"Come," he said as he stood. "Let us go pay respects to my mother until time for dinner to begin." Taking my hand, Skylon led me from the Zenana.

****

The Prince of the Snowy Sky led me through the maze of hallways within the sprawling palace until we stood before two very large wooden doors, carved with lotus flowers and birds. He knocked on the door and then waited as it was opened very slowly from within. A young girl wearing a gold tunic peeked out of the door and smiled brightly as she let us in.

The room within was grand and reminded me much of the welcome parlour at the Painted Lady, with soft couches and chairs and large lounging pillows scattered over the rugs on the floor.

Books lay open on tables and serving trays with the remnants of treats waited near the door to be cleared away. A large archway gilded in gold centred the wall to my left. The wall before us was built with odd angles, much like the top of an octagon, with a set of double doors like those which led to ours in the centre, and a golden door on the angle to either side.

The door to our right opened and a dainty woman of alabaster skin and corn-silk hair stepped out. Her entire front was bare save the belt of her gown riding low on her hips just covering her clean-shaven lotus and her gold jewellery. Her gown was of shimmering gold satin, the high collar just curving about her shoulders enough for long sleeves to attach. The sides of the gown skimmed down to her tiny waist where they joined the ruffled bustle skirt that trailed down the backs of her legs to the floor. A gold sunburst glittered from the centre of her chest just below the hollow of her throat. A golden chain swung between her nipples, and another trailed from her left ear to her nose. A ruby nestled in her naval.

“Mama!” Skylon said as he opened his arms wide and hugged the woman. “This is Celestine.”

We sat and chatted in the family parlour until a servant came for us. I learned that the archway led to the High King's private chambers and that the golden doors led to the Prince of the Rosy Dawn's and the Prince of the Snowy Sky's mothers respectively. As we departed, I paused at the door and looked back, considering.

"What is it dear?" Lady Tanis, the Prince of the Sky's mother, asked.

"I was just wondering why our hall doesn't have such a room. It might help settle things if the Prince of Dawn had private rooms of his own and Antheia had her own space for herself and her ladies. It seems as though the two are perhaps not...well matched." I had offered hesitantly.

"You are an observant one, and after only a few hours of meeting her as well. I shall talk to his mother after dinner tonight."

The dinner had been long, filled with many conversations, many entertainments, and more food than I would generally see in a week back in the caravan. Eventually, the High King stood, took each of his ladies by their hands, and nodded to his sons. The princes arose, kissed their mothers' hands, and bowed to their father before escorting Antheia and myself back to the Zenana.

****

Quietly I slipped from the bed. It amused me that the night-dress I had been provided covered more than the traditional daywear of the Zenana. I could not sleep in this place of jewels and courtesans. Did the ladies of the harems really sit about mostly undressed all day? Many places I had travelled as a dancer had considered their outfits to be highly revealing and the dancing girls had never revealed anything worth seeing without a price being paid. If only those little villages knew about harems!

I passed unnoticed through the bath-house and into the garden. The moon was but a sliver in the dark sky and the stars twinkled. I gazed on the unfamiliar constellations until I found comfort in the constellation we had called Archer. He watched us with his sharp eyes and his enchanted bow ready. I'd always loved the dark of the moon best, for my visions were always strongest when nothing obscured the starlight. Unfortunately, torchlight flourished throughout the gardens and I doubted I would find a dark place to gaze properly.

Turning my back to the moon, and knowing dawn was but a few hours away, I blindly followed a path into the hedgerows with no idea where it would lead. Eventually, I found myself in some sort of maze. Rather afraid of getting lost, or in trouble being out here alone I picked one star to follow and continued forward until the path ended. Before me was a shrine beneath an awning and a well-tended lawn.

A small shelf case stood with various figurines of crystal. I had a passing familiarity with crystals from other fortune tellers we'd met as the dancers travelled with different caravans through the seasons. But what was the purpose of such a shrine within a maze of hedgerows? The crunch of boots on the path startled me, and I tried to hide but knocked into the small case in my hurry and dislodging some of the carvings.

Skylon stepped quickly from the shadows and caught me as I stumbled. "I was worried when you left. I wanted to be sure you were alright."

"I...I couldn't sleep. I thought if I had a walk under the stars, it might relax me. I...I miss the stars. I used to work most of the night, watching the stars, waiting for a vision or sign. I was just waiting for dawn," I replied, still a bit breathless from the scare.

"Were you now?" Skylon looked at her with the hint of a smirk on his face, "I was under the impression that you didn't care for my brother much?"

"What? No, I mean...morning...daylight...." Watching as a grin spread across his face, I pushed him playfully, "You're baiting me."

"I am," he smiled as he kissed my forehead, "but I would enjoy waiting for...the morning with you," he offered, "if you don't mind nought but soft grass for a bed."

"I would cherish a night under the stars with you," I replied, yearning for his touch.

Skylon was gentle as he caressed my face, drawing his fingers down the along my throat as my eyes closed in pleasure.

His lips became more urgent, and I felt his need of me. We slithered into the grass, mouths and hands on one another.

Skylon grinned, "This is a shrine to the god, Marub, Lord of Pleasure. Now I'm beholden to the Goddess but this particular fellow is one of her sons. Dorien is a devotee but I understand these offerings hold some of his particular focus…"

Grinning Skylon reached for one of the egg-shaped jaspers, carved with a square base. He blew on it softly, chilling it, and then began to circle it over across my breasts, teasing my nipples until they were peaks beneath the pale linen nightshirt. Down my body it trailed until Skylon teased it between my legs, slowly moving up and down over my cleft. His mouth was busy with mine, and the sensation built.

As my hips began to move with the rhythm of his hand, Skylon placed my hand over the item, urging me to pleasure myself. "Let it thrill you. Let me watch your pleasure." His voice at my ear was full of desire and together we circled my pip, over the linen. Enough of a touch to bring want and need, but not quite enough to bring relief. His hand stroked downwards, tickling and the cold crystal tingled as it slid slickly. The chill of it made me shiver, and Skylon rolled to kiss me, his hand still rocking the pleasure crystal over my pip. His mouth was on my neck, my exposed skin, and he nipped at me through the linen of my shift. Skylon's warm tongue teased first one, then the other beneath the rough fabric, suckling until the material rubbed and a moan could not be held back. My free arm circled his neck, fingers in his hair as the slow rhythm of the pleasure egg brought me closer to the edge.

His mouth continued to tantalise me as he followed my body, fingers of his free hand slowly inching the nightshirt up and away, a cold night breeze brings a delightful sensation. Lifting my hand, he held the stone before his mouth again, this time warming it before wrapping his tongue around it and then flicking the end. His eyes never left mine.

The stone glistened in the dim light within the garden, and gently pushing my legs further apart he slid the stone into my cleft. All the time my fingers were busy at my pip, and my hips rose and fell.

Skylon's free hand tickled and teased and his hot lips worked their way along my ribs, across my belly and down. He caught my fingers, wet with pleasure and sucked each one. Then his tongue flicked at my cleft as it had at the end of the pleasure crystal. He withdrew the crystal and I cried out, begging for its touch. Skylon laughed, softly, before his mouth settled on my engorged and sensitive pip and teased me further. His hand kept the crystal pumping until I was close to the edge. Then he pulled back, breathing heavily as I moaned and writhed, one hand on the crystal rising and falling and my thumb flicking my pip. In my release I cried out, calling his name and tasting myself on his lips as they brushed mine.

"I see the god pleased you." Skylon's voice was low and full of desire.

"And now, my prince, will you take your release tonight?" I whispered, my breath still fast.

"We still have a while until sun-up," Skylon said with a twinkle in his eye. "But first, I would like to stop at the bath."

****

The Prince of the Sky and I were just preparing to leave the bath-house after our exertions when the Prince of the Dawn strolled in with his ladies. Now, by the looks of the four, you could tell they had been at play for quite some time, and my prince was none too excited to see Dorien parading his courtesans about. Dorien winked at me and the flushed expression I held. Skylon draped a rob about my shoulders, providing some cover.

"I thought you promised your mother that you would spend your nights with your lady wife?" Skylon asked his brother, the displeasure evident in his voice.

"Well, it's not that I didn't try," Dorien replied dismissively. "But seeing's how she still turns me away, and I still have no interest in taking her by force as some have suggested, I sought my pleasures elsewhere."

With a great sigh, Skylon shook his head. "Clean yourself up and let's go talk. Perhaps it is time we took this matter to father instead of leaving it to your mother to solve. Celestine, stay with the others while Dorien and I have a chat."

With a smile and a shrug, I had tossed my towel aside and joined the other girls in the warm water. Now, it has always been my experience, that whenever girls of the sultry arts gather, there's going to be discussion, and whenever the Prince of the Dawn was involved, it was going to be a tale worth hearing, so I should say, that yes, I did encourage them to tell me about their adventures that first night at the palace. This became a regular event and we would exchange tales and suggestions for dealing with and pleasuring our menfolk. This was also how I learned what happened next.

****

Dorien stormed into Lei's room with a fire in his eyes, practically snorting like an angry bull. "Promise bride my backside! So far there's been no promise of anything other than my not getting a proper concubine or secondary wife. If I was a harder man, she'd have begotten me a son by now."

Lei looked up from where she lay on the plush fleece rug on the floor. "If you were a harder man, you'd not seek out willing and trained courtesans to service your needs. Why don't we go to Treela's room so you can blow off some steam? She was going to be giving Felicity lessons tonight."

Dorien's eyebrow lifted, curiosity peaked, and he followed Lei down the hall to Treela's chamber. A large trunk had come with them from the Painted Lady, the latches now off and the lid lifted open. Within rows of long, narrow shelves on a carousel that rotated from top to bottom were filled with the speciality supplies enjoyed by those who favoured the ladies of red and black.

He smiled brightly as he surveyed the room. Familiar red scarves dangled from rings on the walls and buckled cuffs were attached along the baseboards beneath them. The large case stood open, a selection of Dorien's favourite toys displayed on the uppermost shelf tray.

The young prince snickered. "Well now, it seems like maybe you were expecting me?"

Treela grinned. "Not necessarily, as I seem to recall you are meant to be entertaining your promise bride. I had thought to begin training Felicity in the use of props."

"Were you now? I believe that is a lesson I might like to see. Find something that calls to you, something that will give you both pleasure...and then take her, there against the wall while I watch."

"As you wish," Treela smirked, "but you prepare her for me."

Grey eyes locked with hers for a moment before Dorien crossed the room and swept Felicity into a passionate kiss. "Come, my sweet thing. It seems you will have a new lesson this night. I look forward to watching your progress."

He undressed her slowly, opening her bodice one hook at the time as he kissed greedily down her throat to her breasts. He tossed the golden bodice aside as he untied the drawstring of her tunic, letting it slide down her body to pool at her feet. Cupping her breasts, he nuzzled at them until she moaned; then, placing one hand over her cleft, he tantalised her with a touch of magic, pulsing through her as she shivered.

Gently he buckled her ankles into the leather straps fastened to the baseboard of the wall before slowly kissing his way back up her body. He bound her wrists together to a ring above her head with a soft, red scarf as he kissed her.

Lei kissed them each on the cheek and smiled as they turned their heads towards her. "Treela says the lessons may run long. She bids me dose you with the staying powder to enhance your enjoyments."

She held up a white wafer, and Dorien smiled brightly. "I gladly follow my Mistress's command."

Lei placed a wafer onto his tongue before returning to Treela who was still slowly rotating the shelves as though having difficulty finding something that pleased her. As the next shelf rose to the top, Treela smirked as her eyes fell on a gift from Tatia, the Mistress of Black's favoured training tool and toy for her personal lovers.

The shelf was set like a little bed, lined with downy soft pillowing covered with the softest satin. A plush cover was tucked about the item like a little blanket. Slowly Treela pulled the cover back, letting the memories of days in Tatia's chambers flood over her. As her body responded to the memories, she gently caressed the unusual rod.

It looked and felt exactly like a man's member, only twice as long as any man she had ever seen and with a head at either end. At her touch it began to warm, the skin rippling as though muscles beneath were quivering. She blew softly on one end, and the head lifted ever so slightly.

Beside it on the pillow lay a set of black leather straps. Treela disrobed, casting her clothing carelessly aside, and stepped eagerly into the two loops of leather suspended from a belt, slowly sliding them up her legs until she could fasten the belt about her hips. Nestled between the leg straps an odd leather tube lined with fur both inside and out tickled at her pip.

With great care, she lifted the rod, raising one head to her lips, she kissed it softly and whispered, "Pleasure me and I shall pleasure you. The pleasure of my partner, my gift to you."

The skin surrounding the head began to quiver, and she rolled it back softly, licking to tip before taking it into her mouth. The colour began to slowly change from soft flesh tones to grey, the girth subtly increasing as she sucked.

Dorien stepped behind her, nibbling at her ear. "What have you there my sweet?"

"A pleasure pet, a personal gift from Tatia. She took apprentices only rarely, and personal lovers even less frequently. There were few who could sate her desires. I think she was sad to see me go."

With a wave of her hand, Lei took the rod and knelt before Treela, sliding the rod into the little sling before inserting the swollen, grey end into her cleft; the gift calling to the magic in her blood, heightening her senses.

Leading her back to the wall, Dorien bit her throat as he spanked Treela's bare behind. The exquisite pain of his playful bite and slap shot through her, amplified by the magic, the rod almost seeming to vibrate from it. She ran her hands slowly over Felicity as Dorien stepped away, tracing the curves of her tiny waist, up to her full breasts, along her slender arms. Cupping her face Treela kissed her, softly at first, and then with a hunger as the rod pulsed within her, amplifying her need. Breasts pressed together, Lei pushed the warm rod into Felicity's cleft with an agonising slowness as the gift seemed to grow, filling them both with its girth until they gasped at the size of it, the rod reading its new mistress and shaping itself as the member of a full troll male for her and as a muscular desert warrior for her partner.

Seemingly of its own accord, the rod began to sway between the two girls in a slow, steady rhythm. After a short time, Treela picked up the rhythm, pumping her hips to drive the thrusts deeper for both.

Dorien lounged on a soft chair draped in red watching as Treela serviced Felicity. Lei was curled on the floor before him wearing her gold dress from the Painted Lady, stroking his member as the herbs slowly took effect. He maintained the code of the Lady and did not touch Lei while she worked.

As the full force of the herbs kicked in, his need for contact became a hunger that was almost a physical pain. With a small hand motion from him, Lei stopped her attentions and brought him a tray of balms. As the sounds of Felicity's moans intensified, so did his hunger, and a low growl rumbled in his throat as Lei coated his swollen, throbbing member with a warming balm.

Dorien's deepest desire at that moment was to take Felicity, almost as if a spell had him enraptured to ravage her, such was the power of the herbs, but Treela stood in the way of his prize, the pleasure pet having them fully in its thrall as if fed on their pleasure.

Placing his hands firmly on Treela's hips, he entered her from the rear, her high-pitched gasping moan slowly fading to a panting as his magic called to the toy. He stood for a time simply feeling the pulsing of the toy, the warmth as it rocked through her, and he pressed his face into her hair just letting the sensations wash over him.

Dorien groaned as the toy rubbed against him through the thin wall of tissue separating them. Treela sighed, wrapping her leg around Felicity's, who moaned along with them. Treela reached up and grabbed the ring as Dorien began to thrust, her cheek pressed against Felicity's. The girls hung there panting together, the magic pulsing through them until Treela and Felicity cried out as one, shuddering all over as Lei kissed them each softly.

Ever so gently Lei removed the pleasure pet, cold shivers covering both girls as the magic ebbed away. As Lei carried the rod to the wash basin, Dorien caught Treela as her legs gave way, carrying her to the nearby bed. Then he returned for Felicity, gently untying her and carrying her to the bed as well.

****

Stories never take as long to recount as an event took to live, so it really wasn't all that long before we wandered back towards our rooms wrapped in fluffy towels, only to be greeted by the unmistakable sounds of a heated argument coming from behind the double doors to the common room.

****

"I will not be spied upon by my old matron in my own Zenana. I am not a child in a communal nursery any longer, and I will not have my mother fetched to chide me each time I do something that might displease her. I am the heir to the high throne, and I demand to be treated as such!" Dorien yelled as he tossed a small pedestal down, smashing an antique vase in the process.

"You demand?!" his old matron scoffed. "You demand? You are throwing a hissy fit like a little girl, that is what you are doing. 'I'm a man now,' indeed. You are a raunchy youth sowing his wild oats and bonking every floozy that bares her chest or hikes her skirt. You beget yourself an heir with your rightful bride so your father can place his seal on that scroll of fealty from the colony across the sea, and then I might let you think yourself a man. Your grandfather, now he was a man who could demonstrate why he was High King. Took the firstborn daughter of every clan patriarch for himself..."

"Enough!" Dorien's mother Tyra called as the double doors entering the Zenana banged loudly against the walls. She was flanked on either side by armed temple guards, and the armourer stood behind her holding a box. A young girl dressed in a servant's tunic cowered in the hallway.

"I do not believe the High King wishes to return to the practices of the past to fulfil the terms of fealty promises," Tyra said to the matron scornfully. "But I do agree that the promise must be fulfilled.

"Both of you will be confined to the eastern suite until such time you resolve your... differences. They are large, and you may have separate chambers, but you will eat together, bathe together and you WILL do what is necessary. Once the heir is confirmed you may take your pleasures where you wish."

She glared at her son, "There are other lords, other princelings, beget from the harem. Keep that in mind and recall your history - for the minor lord, Aristus, son of a handmaiden was raised to be heir when his brothers were disinherited. It has been known."

With a wry smile, she looked around the room, recalling her own arrival some twenty-odd years ago, "Sex and power are linked, remember that. For the strongest man may yield to a whispered promise or a shapely form, and the lowliest feel like a king in the arms of his lover. Your duty must ALWAYS come first and sometimes pleasure must make way for duty."

****

So passed my months in the secluded luxury of the Zenana, for it is a cossetted and closeted life. Skylon would come to me, and for me. Seldom he took his pleasures elsewhere but we both knew his bride would be the goddess and his palace the temple and it could never be more than what it was. We loved one another, I think, yet there was sadness with the pleasure as it could not last beyond a summer or two. Skylon even approached his father, and the temple to have me by his side or to release him from his vow. Not even the High King dared to revoke such an ancient rite, and so my prince would fulfil his destiny, and mine would be apart from his, so the stars foresaw, and the goddess blessed us both.

Dorien eventually did his duty, and a young prince was born to him, but when I left those rosy hours he still preferred to seek his fun elsewhere than his lady's bed and she, well, she found comfort with her handmaidens. For such were her tastes.

The carriage which bore me away from that realm gleamed in the summer sun, crystal and silver as the tears in my eyes. I wondered if he watched from the temple. Without my prince, I was alone, in that court of pleasure, though there were plenty for company he I longed for could not be mine. Even now I recall the tears we shed for a life which could not be. But the heart heals. For the stars have shown me wealth, love, loss, power and magic and that time brings other lovers, other adventures to be had, and other lives to be lived. I took but one thing with me when I left that land, his golden mask.

Epilogue

Seraphina glanced up at the golden mask that hung above the chamber door. "The adventures you have seen," she mused. Seraphina knew passion and desire were the same for highborn and lowborn alike. "When a man stands before me in nothing but his skin I care not if he is prince or pauper, for all may be equal in the bedchamber. Sex is power. Desire is influence. That is what matters." With a sweeping gesture, she settled the mask on her face. "Now I am complete."

Gently she closed the book and placed it back into its hiding place. "I'll return to you my friend, do not doubt that. And perhaps I'll add my own chapter."

The door swung shut on the chambers of the most sought-after woman in the land. Further tales could wait for another day.

Alexa Lynsey and Belle De Ver write fantasy as their other selves.

If you ask them nicely, they may reveal other stories and other worlds.

Please look out for more *Tales of the Golden Mask.*

To follow the authors please visit https://www.facebook.com/Alexalynseyauthor/ *for Golden Mask news, interviews and chat or* https://twitter.com/GoldenMask17